My Grandma's the Mayor

To Mom and Dad, who gave me the gift of service — MWP

Published by MAGINATION PRESS, An Educational Publishing Foundation Book
American Psychological Association
750 First Street, NE, Washington, DC 20002

For more information about our books, including a complete catalog, please write to us, call 1-800-374-2721, or visit our website at www.maginationpress.com.

Editor: Darcie Conner Johnston   The text type is Bodoni Light
Art Director: Susan K. White   Printed by Phoenix Color, Rockaway, New Jersey

Library of Congress Cataloging-in-Publication Data

Pellegrino, Marjorie White.
My grandma's the mayor / by Marjorie White Pellegrino ; illustrated by John Lund.
p. cm.
Summary: Annie is unhappy that she has to share her grandmother, the mayor, with so many people, but when she helps out during a town emergency, Annie appreciates all that her grandmother does in the community.
ISBN 1-55798-608-8 (alk. paper)
[1. Grandmothers Fiction. 2. Mayors Fiction. 3. City and town life Fiction.]
I. Lund, John (John H.), ill. II. Title.
PZ7.P3637My 1999
[Fic]-dc21   99-16771
                             CIP

Manufactured in the United States of America
10 9 8 7 6 5 4 3 2 1

My Grandma's THE MAYOR

by
Marjorie White Pellegrino

illustrated by
John Lund

MAGINATION PRESS • WASHINGTON, DC

My grandma is different from other grandmas. It's not just because she's shorter than most, or because she's actually proud that her hair is completely white.

She's different because she went and got herself elected as the mayor. Now she's mostly too busy to spend much time with me.

But it wasn't always that way. We used to have whole "Annie and Grandma" days together. We'd start off at Pauline's Bakery, eating cookies and talking about school and my friends. Sometimes we'd go to the park and feed the ducks and play catch. After dinner, we always took a walk with Grandpa and we would trade jokes, or sometimes we'd stay in and play board games. And always at bedtime, after we'd read, Grandma would tell me funny stories about my mom when she was just my age.

Now that Grandma's the mayor, everything is different.

At first I wanted her to be the mayor. I even helped her get the job. I passed out flyers, helped put up signs, and stuffed envelopes for her campaign. I thought all she would have to do was ride on a float in the parade next summer, be on television, and lead the Pledge of Allegiance. And then I could say, "That's my Grandma. She's the mayor."

But I've changed my mind. Now that my Grandma got elected, I don't think it's such a good idea. I'll tell you why.

Grandma isn't just the mayor when there's a meeting or a parade. Like this one time, we were outside playing catch in her backyard, and I heard the phone ring. She took the phone out of her pocket and put her other hand up like a police officer to tell me to stop throwing the ball to her. Then she walked away. So much for our game!

It doesn't matter where we are. When we're in Pauline's Bakery or Crestwood Pharmacy or Epstein's Clothes, people stop her and say things like, "Did you hear about the health fair?" or "You better get somebody out to fix that sign on Stewart Avenue." When we go to feed the ducks, everyone waves and says hello to her. Sometimes I feel like I'm invisible.

My whole family always has Thursday night pizza at Roma's. Now people come up to our table and say, "Oh Mayor, how are you?" and "We need you at the community center meeting next Tuesday" or whatever. Yackety, yackety, yack! We get interrupted so much that Grandma's food gets cold. But the interrupting isn't the worst part. Once when we were taking a walk, Mrs. Lufa stopped us and told Grandma about how fast cars zoom past her apartment house. Her voice got louder and louder, and she sounded really mad. I wanted to tell her to stop talking to Grandma like that, but I was too scared.

"She wasn't really yelling at me, Annie," Grandma said, and she gave me a hug. "She's just upset about the cars. She has a problem, and it's my job to help people find ways to solve problems." Grandma doesn't even yell back. I would if I were the mayor.

Mom says I should try and look at the bright side. Okay, I guess there are some good things about Grandma being the mayor. Like when I visit her office and she's not too busy, she takes me downstairs to the police station. If the jail cells are empty, she even lets me lock her in.

Sometimes when Grandma cuts the ribbon at a new store, she takes me along, and I get my picture in the newspaper.

Last summer I got to see drawings of the new playground at the park before anyone at school did.

And once when there was a blizzard, Grandma rode in the snowplow to see how many trees had fallen down and how slippery the streets were. She had the driver beep the horn when they rode past our house. That was one time I wished I could be the mayor!

When Mom and I walk over to the library Friday after school, I tell her I do like some things about Grandma's new job, but I still miss the way it used to be. "When will Grandma be done being mayor?" I ask.

"Not for a long time," Mom says and squeezes my hand. "Maybe what you need is an Annie-Grandma sleepover." I think Mom is right!

Mom calls Grandma as soon as we get home. I can hardly believe it! Tonight Grandma was supposed to have a meeting, but now the meeting's going to be next week because someone important got sick. She says I can come over as soon as I want to. It takes me exactly one minute to stuff my pajamas and toothbrush in my backpack.

At Grandma and Grandpa's house we have
my favorite dinner, macaroni and cheese, and we
get to eat it while it's hot because there's no one to
interrupt. I help with the dishes, and then Grandma
and I put together a puzzle that's really hard but
fun. While we're working, the phone rings twice.
Grandpa takes messages so Grandma can listen
to my plans for my science project.

I snuggle in bed under Grandma's special circle
quilt, the one that looks like a rainbow of hugs,
and we talk about going to Pauline's Bakery in the
morning. Grandma kisses me goodnight and says,
"Did I tell you about the time your mom kissed
Grandpa when he had shaving cream all over
his face?"

As I fall asleep, I think about how good it is to
have Grandma back all to myself.

In the middle of a dream, I hear a loud boom. It doesn't sound like thunder or anything else I've ever heard, and suddenly I know I'm not dreaming.

"Grandma! Grandpa," I shout, and I throw back my covers and run into their room.

Grandpa is looking out the window and putting on his coat over his pajamas.

Grandma is on the phone. She's saying, "Fire… sounded like an explosion."

She pulls on her jeans and tucks her nightgown in like a shirt, and while she's still talking she hugs me close. Her arms are warm. They make me feel less afraid.

Through the window I can see flames shooting out of the apartment house across the street. There's Grandpa, running toward the building, and all kinds of people are rushing outside in their pajamas. Some people have their arms around each other, and some are carrying little kids. Mrs. Lufa is crying so loud I can hear her through Grandma's closed window. I hear sirens too, getting closer and closer, and all at once two fire trucks come roaring up. The firefighters jump off and yell to each other while they hook up hoses to the fire hydrant.

Just then Grandma hangs up the phone. "We've got to get moving," she says gently, but I can tell she means business. I get my jeans and coat on quicker than I ever did in my whole life, and help Grandma pull the blankets off the beds before we leave.

"We have to get those people out of the cold," Grandma says as we run outside. She puts a blanket around Mrs. Lufa's shoulders and hands out the others until we don't have any more. Pretty soon people follow her like a raggedy dream parade down the street toward the community center.

Grandma knocks on the door. The custodian looks confused when he sees all of us in the dark. But Grandma calls him over to the door and talks to him real soft like she does to me when I fall down or somebody calls me names.

Finally he unlocks the door. People pour in out of the cold. Before Grandma can even get her coat off, she picks up the phone. Between calls she tells people which closet holds the folding chairs and how to start up the big coffeepot.

After a while, Mr. Epstein sends over socks, sweatsuits, and slippers from his store. Mrs. Chin brings medicines from her pharmacy that people didn't have time to take from their apartments. John from Roma's brings in big trays of hot food, and Pauline brings rolls and bread and cookies.

Grandma helps dish out the meals and hugs the people who look afraid and sad. With some people she laughs, because they are all so happy no one was hurt. Grandma knows just how to make everyone feel better.

I start to think about what I can do to help, like Grandma does.

I've got it! I run up to Grandpa, who is helping John from Roma's clear off tables. "Can you please take me home?" I ask. "I want to get some stuff for the kids so they'll have something to do besides think about the fire." "That's a plan, Annie," he says, and we're out the door as soon as we can get our coats on.

I make so much noise running into the house that Mom and Dad wake up.

"What's going on?" asks Dad in the hallway. He and Mom are trying to get their robes on. I don't realize I'm yelling when I tell them about the loud explosion and the fire right across the street from Grandma and Grandpa's house until Grandpa puts his hand on my shoulder. He says in his calm voice to Mom and Dad, who look kind of worried, "Everything is fine. The situation is all under control." He tells Mom about the community center while Dad helps me get some board games and books.

The sun is starting to come up as we load the car. "Look," I show him, "it's a new day!"

"That turned out to be some sleepover!"
says Mom later, after Grandpa brings me home
again. I laugh, even though I am still a little sad
about losing my special time with Grandma.
"At first I was scared about the fire, and then
I was a little mad, and then I wanted to cry,"
I tell her, "but it turned out okay."

"What made it okay?" Mom asks gently, like she
might already know the answer.

"I think because I got to help," I say. "It felt the
way I feel when I get an A in a hard class at
school, maybe even better than that. But I still
want to have an Annie-Grandma time again soon!"

"I think that's a good idea," Mom laughs.

That night when I snuggle in my own bed, I think
about Grandma. I know she can't always play
games with me and do things other grandmas do,
because she has meetings and mayor work.
I share Grandma with a lot of people, but I don't
mind it too much now.

At the next village meeting, Grandma lets me hold the fancy certificates called proclamations for the people who helped during the fire. I hand one to her, and she calls the person up in front of the room and shakes hands.

Everybody claps. When I hand her the last proclamation she reads my name!

I look up into Grandma's eyes while everyone is clapping, and she's shaking my hand. I can tell Grandma is proud of me and all the people in her community.

And I am really proud of my Grandma.
My Grandma, the mayor.

ABOUT THE AUTHOR

Marjorie White Pellegrino grew up in Tuckahoe, New York, in a home where everyone volunteered in the community. Her dad has served in elective office for more than 30 years. She knows that sometimes it's hard to share the ones you love with so many other people. But she also knows the good feeling you get when you help the place where you live become even better.

Marge has lived in Tucson, Arizona, since 1979. In the organizations she volunteers for, the words she writes, and the workshops she teaches, she tries to build a spirit of community. She is the author of *I Don't Have an Uncle Phil Anymore*, a book for children about death and grieving, published by MAGINATION PRESS.